DORRIE
and the Fortune Teller

written and illustrated by
Patricia Coombs

GO AWAY

NO SPYING

Lothrop, Lee & Shepard Company / New York

This is Dorrie. She is a witch. A little witch. Her hat is always on crooked and her socks never match. Dorrie lives in Witchville with her black cat Gink, and her mother, the Big Witch, and Cook.

One night a strange-looking wagon stopped on a hill above Witchville. A window swung open on the side. Something long and thin came out the window. The moonlight shone on it as it pointed toward Witchville. Then the window closed, and the wagon came down the hill and behind some trees.

No one in Witchville saw the wagon. All the witches and wizards were tossing and turning in their beds.

For weeks they had tried to raise enough money to buy their meadow and the Town Tower that they rented from the Wizard Floog. They had twelve hours left. If they didn't have the money, Floog would take over the meadow and the Tower for a Tar and Cigar Factory.

The next morning, Dorrie woke up early. She climbed out of bed and got dressed. She looked out the window.

"Gink," said Dorrie, "we've just got to find a way to keep our meadow and. . . ." Dorrie stopped. She stared down at the yard. There were white squares stuck all over the trees and posts.

"Hmmm," said Dorrie, "I wonder what those things are."

Down, down, down the stairs went Dorrie, and Gink went with her. Out the door they ran and into the yard.

"Posters! Someone must have stuck them here last night while we were asleep. We'll take one in to Mother."

Down the hall she went, and into the kitchen. Cook was mumbling and grumbling and stirring a pot of mush. The Big Witch was pouring a cup of coffee and looking *very* worried.

"Mother! Cook!" said Dorrie. "Guess what?"

"I never guess before breakfast," said the Big Witch, crossly. "And your hat is wrong-side out."

"Look," said Dorrie, waving the poster. "These are stuck all over the trees and posts."

"I don't want to look," groaned the Big Witch. "They are probably notices from Floog that we have just twelve hours left before he takes over the meadow and the Tower."

The Big Witch sighed and took the poster from Dorrie. Her eyes popped wide open and she read aloud:

MADAME ZEE! WORLD-FAMOUS FORTUNE TELLER! WILL GIVE READINGS AT THE WITCHVILLE TOWN TOWER 5 P.M. TO MIDNIGHT. TEA LEAVES READ. PALMS READ. CARDS READ. THE FUTURE FORETOLD. REASONABLE PRICES.

The Big Witch clapped her hands. "Good news for a change! Madame Zee in Witchville. What luck! I've heard how helpful and kind she is. She can foresee Witchville's fate, and tell us what we must do! Quick, Dorrie, my boots! My broomstick!"

Dorrie ran and got the Big Witch's boots and broomstick.

"I must fly into town right away, and tell the Tower Committee to clean the Tower. And tell the Tea-and-Cakes Committee and the Banner-and-Balloon Committee and. . . ."

"I'll come with you," said Dorrie. "Gink and I will help."

"NO!" cried the Big Witch. "You'll be in the way. This is the biggest event in Witchville in a hundred years. It will change everything. You go and be sure that the witches and wizards on the other side of the meadow have seen the posters. Tell them they *must* come. And be sure you are back early."

"All right," said Dorrie.

With a swish and a leap, the Big Witch flew off on her broomstick.

Dorrie and Gink ate breakfast and said goodbye to Cook.

Across the yard they went, and down the road and up a hill. Dorrie could see witches and wizards flying all around the Town Tower like blackbirds. Other witches and wizards were leaning out of windows, shaking the moths and dust from their best clothes.

"Gink," said Dorrie, "if Floog puts a factory there, it'll be so black and smoky nobody will be able to fly his broomstick anymore. The pumpkins will shrivel up and spells won't work. I hope Madame Zee can help."

Dorrie and Gink walked through the meadow. They stopped at the Egg Witch's house and told her about Madame Zee. They went to Mr. Obs's house and all the others on that side of the meadow.

On the way back, Dorrie and Gink sat on a stone to rest. Dorrie looked toward the trees beyond the fence. Something moved in the shadows. It moved again.

MADAME
WORLD FAMOUS
FORTUNE TOLD
WITCHVILLE
TOWN SQUARE
5 p.m. & 12
PALMS READ
TEA LEAVE
REASONABLE
RATES

"Come on, Gink," Dorrie said. "Let's go see what's over there. I thought everybody was at the Town Tower or busy getting ready."

Dorrie and Gink went in among the trees. Closer and closer and closer. Suddenly there was a snort.

Dorrie jumped. "A horse! Oh, my, an old gray horse and a house on wheels! I never saw anything like this before."

Dorrie went closer. She looked at all the signs and symbols painted on the sides of the wagon. A machine with a long pipe was sticking out of one of the windows. Dorrie stood on tiptoe and looked into it.

"YOW!" yelled Dorrie, and her hat fell off. An eye was glaring back at her from the other end of the pipe. The eye disappeared. So did the machine. Then the window swung shut with a bang and the door opened. An angry witch with gold earrings came storming out.

"Why are you snooping and spying on me?" snarled the witch. "Go away! And DON'T COME BACK! I turn snoopers into moles and weasels!" Waving her broomstick, the witch chased Dorrie away from the wagon. Then she rushed around, tacking signs to the trees. They said:

DO NOT DISTURB! GO AWAY! BEWARE!
NO SNOOPING! NO SPYING! DANGER!

Dorrie and Gink ran into the woods. Dorrie stopped to look back through the trees at the wagon.

"Hmph!" said Dorrie. "That's the maddest, mean-est witch I ever saw! If I had a wagon like that I'd like people to look at it. I'd have them in for tea and show them how everything works."

The sky was getting darker and the wind blew leaves around them.

"Hurry, Gink," said Dorrie. "It's getting late and we were supposed to be home early. We have to get ready to have our fortunes told."

Dorrie and Gink ran home and into the kitchen.

"Cook!" called Dorrie. "Where are you?"

"Taking a bubble bath!" shouted Cook. "Your sandwich and milk are on the table. Hurry and get ready!"

"Where's Mother?"

"Ironing her cloak!" yelled Cook.

Dorrie ate her sandwich and drank her milk.

She gave Gink some milk. Then they ran up, up, up the stairs.

Dorrie washed and changed her dress.

Down, down, down the stairs she went, and Gink went with her.

The Big Witch rushed into the hall. She put on her cloak and got out her best broomstick. She looked at Dorrie. "WHERE IS YOUR HAT?" cried the Big Witch. "You can't go to the Town Tower without your hat!"

"Oh, no!" said Dorrie. "It must have fallen off when that witch chased me. It's still in the woods. I'll be right back."

"What witch? What woods? I can't wait for you!" cried the Big Witch. "I want to be the first to have my fortune told!"

"I'll go with Cook," said Dorrie, and she ran out the door.

The Big Witch flew off to the Town Tower.

Dorrie and Gink ran back into the woods toward the wagon.

"Shhh," said Dorrie. "We have to be very, VERY quiet, Gink. We don't want that witch to know we're here."

Dorrie looked and looked for her hat. Around and around and around the wagon she went. It wasn't any use. The hat wasn't there. And the wagon was very, very quiet.

Dorrie went closer. She peeked into one of the windows.

"There's a little stove, and a bed, and a bench and—my hat! It's right there! The witch doesn't seem to be around, so I'll just run inside and grab it."

Dorrie pushed open the door. She looked in to be sure the witch wasn't there, and then she went inside and got her hat. She pulled it on. Then she saw the strange machine sticking out a window.

"Hmm," said Dorrie. "I'll just take one look through this thing before we go, Gink."

Dorrie looked through it. "It's pointing right at Witchville, at the Town Tower! That's funny, it just shows *metal*. Doorknobs and latches and pipes and the furnace and . . . and . . . oh my goodness! A metal chest and it's all shiny and golden treasure! Buried treasure!"

Dorrie stood back and looked at the side of the machine. It said: *Madame Zee's Treasure Detector.*

"Madame Zee? That mean witch is Madame Zee? Mother said she was kind and helpful. I bet she's going to help herself to that treasure before Floog takes over the Town Tower. Quick, Gink, we've got to run and tell mother."

Cook had already flown off to the Tower. Dorrie and Gink ran all the way. When they got to the Tower the last of the witches and wizards were waiting to have their fortunes told.

WELCOME TO WITCHVILLE
MADAME ZEE

The Big Witch was in another room, pouring tea.
A big banner hung over the room. It said:

WELCOME TO WITCHVILLE, MADAME ZEE

Witches and wizards were all drinking tea and
talking excitedly.

"Mother," whispered Dorrie. "I have to tell you something very important. It's about Madame Zee. I don't think she's a real Fortune Teller at all!"

The Big Witch smiled. "Don't be silly, dear. Wait until you hear what Madame Zee told me!"

"Did she tell you about the treasure buried under the Town Tower?" said Dorrie.

"Buried treasure? Under the Tower?" The Big Witch felt Dorrie's head. "I think you're feverish. The excitement probably. Sit down and listen. Poor Witchville is doomed. There is going to be a terrible earthquake. But before it happens, we will all move to a place called Zeeville. Madame Zee foresees riches and journeys. She says everything will turn out well."

"But Mother," said Dorrie.

"Run along now and have your fortune told. You'll feel better. At midnight there will be a big, important meeting with Madame Zee."

Dorrie went out into the hall. "Come on, Gink," she said. "There's only one way to find out for sure if Madame Zee and that witch are the same person."

Around a corner they went, and down another hall behind the room where Madame Zee was telling fortunes. Dorrie found a closet and slipped inside. There was a hole in one of the boards. Dorrie could look right into the room and hear everything Madame Zee was saying.

"That's her all right," whispered Dorrie. "That mean witch IS Madame Zee."

Madame Zee wore a long dress and had scarves wound around her head. Her gold earrings glittered in the candlelight. A wizard came in and sat down in front of her.

"I, the great Madame Zee, will read your future. Give me your hand."

The wizard held out his hand.

"I see . . . ooh, ohhh!" cried Madame Zee, putting her hand over her eyes. "It is too terrible! I cannot tell you!"

"But you must!" cried the wizard. "I must know!"

"News that bad costs another two dollars," said Madame Zee. "It is so hard on my nerves."

"Yes, yes," said the wizard, putting more money on the table.

Madame Zee told the wizard the same things she had told the Big Witch. She told everyone exactly the same things. There was going to be a terrible earthquake and they must all leave Witchville.

Dorrie tiptoed out of the closet. "We've got to get to work—fast. There is only one thing to do. Mother didn't believe me, and nobody else will either. We have to dig up the treasure before midnight, Gink. Once they see the treasure, they'll see they're being tricked."

Dorrie found the door to the cellar and down, down, down the dark stairs they went.

"Now," said Dorrie. "The Treasure Detector showed the furnace, and about three feet to the left and underneath is the chest."

Dorrie measured off three feet. She knelt down and looked. There were two flat stones that didn't match the rest. Dorrie wriggled her fingers under them and lifted them up.

"I need a shovel to dig with, Gink. I bet there's one in the coal bin."

Dorrie swung open the door to the coal bin and peered into the dark.

"YOW!" yelled Dorrie. A pair of legs and waving feet were hanging from the end of the coal chute.

"HELP!" cried a muffled voice from inside the chute. "HELP ME! I'M STUCK!"

"Who's in there?" said Dorrie.

"Floog! I was listening by the window to find out if Witchville had raised the money. I slipped and fell into the chute. Save me!"

"I'll help you if you'll help me," said Dorrie.

"I promise," said Floog. "Get the tin snips!"

Dorrie ran and got the tin snips. She climbed up on the coal pile and began to snip away at the chute. As she snipped she told Floog about Madame Zee and the buried treasure.

"And," said Dorrie, "by the time everybody discovers they've been tricked, it'll be too late. She'll have run off with the treasure. You'll have the meadow and the Tower. And we won't have anything except a lot of smoke and racket!"

"That's rotten!" cried Floog. "That's cheating! And stealing! She's even rottener than I am!"

Dorrie finally got the chute cut away from around the top of Floog.

"There," said Dorrie. "We haven't time to get the rest of it from around your middle. I can hear everybody going into the main room for the big meeting right now! Come on!"

Dorrie grabbed the shovel and dug the dirt away from the chest. She tugged and pulled and got it out of the hole.

"It's too heavy for me to carry alone," said Dorrie, "and your arms are still stuck. Oh, dear!"

"Quick, take off your socks and tie them together around one handle. Stick the ends of the socks up under the chute and I'll grab them," said Floog.

In a flash, Dorrie pulled off her socks and tied them together and around the handle. She gave the ends to Floog, and together they puffed their way up, up, up the stairs.

Down the hall they went to the back of the stage.

They looked in. Madame Zee was waving her arms and shouting, "You must leave Witchville at once! Before it is too late!"

"Dorrie!" whispered Floog. "I once saw the *real* Madame Zee. This witch is a fake!"

All the witches and wizards were leaping up to leave. Madame Zee was shouting, "SAVE YOURSELVES!"

"SAVE YOUR BREATH!" roared Floog. He and Dorrie rushed out onto the stage with the chest.

The witches and wizards all stopped in their tracks with a gasp.

"This witch is tricking Witchville into leaving so she can dig up the gold she knew was buried here! LOOK!" Dorrie flung open the chest in front of everyone. Gold shimmered in the candlelight.

With a wild screech, the fake Madame Zee leaped toward the gold.

"Oh, no, you don't," roared Floog, and he threw himself on the floor and rolled into the witch and sent her flying. She scrambled to her feet and leaped out a window.

"After her!" yelled Dorrie. "We have to get the Treasure Detector from the wagon before she does!"

Out the window went the Big Witch and Dorrie. They leaped onto a broomstick and flew after Madame Zee. Dorrie showed the Big Witch the grove of trees where the wagon was hidden and they dove down. The witch was just racing back to her broomstick with the Treasure Detector when the Big Witch grabbed her by the ankles. Dorrie grabbed the Treasure Detector.

The Big Witch tweaked the witch's nose. "Where is the real Madame Zee? What have you done with her?"

"ENNNH! Under the bench in the wagon! Ennnh! Eeeh!" With a wild kick at the Big Witch, the witch leaped to her broomstick and disappeared over the hill.

Dorrie went inside the wagon and lifted the lid of the chest. There was the real Madame Zee, all tied up. Dorrie untied her and got her a drink of water.

"Oh, thank you! Thank you!" cried Madame Zee.

All the other witches and wizards had flown down around the wagon.

Madame Zee told them how she had heard of Witchville's trouble. She had been on her way with the Treasure Detector to see if she could help when she was tricked by the witch.

"Thanks to Dorrie," said Madame Zee, "Witchville is saved and so am I! She was the only one who saw what was happening. That is always better than seeing what *may* happen!"

The witches and wizards all shouted and cheered: "Witchville is saved! The meadow and Tower are ours forever! Hurrah for Dorrie!"

And they all flew back to the Town Tower, laughing and cheering.

BLACK POND
WITCH MEADOW

They snipped Floog out of the rest of the coal chute and brushed him off.

Floog bowed and thanked them. "Thank you," said Floog. "If Dorrie hadn't found me stuck in the chute in the cellar, I might have been there forever!" Floog wiped a tear from his eye. "I'm sorry that I ever thought of doing anything to make Witchville unhappy!"

The Big Witch counted out the gold for Floog and gave it to him.

Then they had a big party, with hot tea and cookies and cakes. It was a REAL welcome for the REAL Madame Zee. They danced and sang all through the Tower in a long parade with balloons and candles.

The Big Witch and Dorrie and Gink flew Madame Zee home to the wagon.

"Tomorrow, before I leave," said Madame Zee, "Dorrie and I will ride all around Witchville in the wagon. We will mark the places where more gold may still be buried.

Then the Big Witch and Dorrie and Gink climbed back on the broomstick and flew home to bed.

Dorrie yawned and pulled the covers up under her chin. "Someday maybe we'll live in a wagon, Gink. With a fat gray horse to pull it around. And lots and lots of black cats."

Dorrie fell sound asleep, and so did Gink.